POM POM
the Champion

PUFFIN

by
Sophy Henn

One morning Pom Pom was all
at sixes and sevens.

He didn't know **what** to do with himself.

"Shall we play a game, dear?"
asked Pom Pom's mummy.

"YES!" said Pom Pom.
"I love playing games."

"...6...7...8... Yay!
I'm the WINNER!"
said Pom Pom.

And Pom Pom realized he rather
liked being the winner.

So, he won at NOT being
the tallest or the shortest . . .

He was FIRST to
finish elevenses . . .

And then he won at being the **first**
to get ready to go out.

"I'm the winner!"
said Pom Pom.

At the supermarket Pom Pom packed
his shopping bag the **fastest**.

Emplayee of the Week

"I'm the winner!"
said Pom Pom.

In the library Pom Pom was
the first to finish his book.

"I'm the winner!"
said Pom Pom.

"*Shhhhh,*" said the librarian.

At the park Pom Pom was up the steps
and down the slide . . .

all before his baby brother,
Boo Boo, was even out
of his pushchair.

"I'm the WINNER!"
said Pom Pom.

"Hey, want to play scooters
with us?" asked Baxter.

"YES!" said Pom Pom. "But I'd better tell you I am just winning at everything today . . .

Bet you CAN'T catch me!"

"oh."

"I know," said Rocco.
"Let's play on the swings."

"Yes!" said Pom Pom.
"I bet I can win at 'who can
go the **highest**'."

"oh."

"Shall we play on the
climbing frame next?" asked Buddy.

"Yes!" said Pom Pom. "Let's see who can get to the top of the climbing frame FIRST. Bet it's me!"

"oh."

"Never mind," said Rocco.
"It's just for fun."

"Come on, let's play
catch," said Scout.

"Yes!" said Pom Pom.
"I ALWAYS win at catch . . ."

But Pom Pom **didn't** win at catch.

"That's IT!" yelled Pom Pom.
"It's NOT fair! I'm a winner!
I'm going to GO and WIN
on
my
OWN!"

And that's just what Pom Pom did.

He won at running.

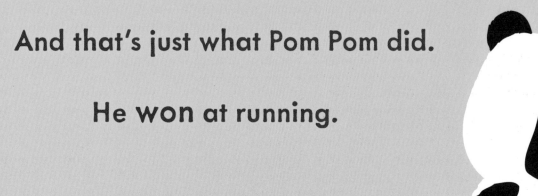

He won at superhero poses.

And he won a dance-off.

But even with all that winning
Pom Pom didn't feel
very happy at all.

Something was missing.

"All right?" asked Scout.
"Are you having fun winning?"

"Not really," said Pom Pom.

"Then come and play with us," said Scout.
"We're having a race."

"Yes, but I'll **probably** win," said Pom Pom.
"And I'm not so sure I like winning any more."

"Oh, don't worry about that . . ."
said the others.

"We can ALL win together!"

And they did.

For Maisie and Kit
Super Champions!
x x   x   x   x

the end

PUFFIN BOOKS
UK | USA | Canada | Ireland | Australia | India | New Zealand | South Africa
Puffin Books is part of the Penguin Random House group of companies
whose addresses can be found at global.penguinrandomhouse.com.
puffinbooks.com
First published 2015
001
Text and illustrations copyright © Sophy Henn, 2015
The moral right of the author/illustrator has been asserted
A CIP catalogue record for this book is available from the British Library
Made and printed in China
Hardback ISBN: 978–0–723–29983–7
Paperback ISBN: 978–0–723–29984–4